THIS BLOOMSBURY BOOK

BELONGS TO

....

To Meg, Duncan & Kate,
whose engines roar 90 mph all day long
K.D.

To G. Brian Karas,
with thanks to the first Mini Racer fan!
B.S.-M.

Bloomsbury Publishing, London, Berlin, New York and Sydney

First published in Great Britain in February 2011 by Bloomsbury Publishing Plc
36 Soho Square, London, W1D 3QY

Text copyright © Kristy Dempsey 2011
Illustrations copyright © Bridget Strevens-Marzo 2011
The moral rights of the author and illustrator have been asserted

A CIP catalogue record of this book is available from the British Library

ISBN 978 1 4088 0038 6

FSC
www.fsc.org
MIX
Paper from
responsible sources
FSC® C008047

Printed in China by C & C Offset Printing Co Ltd, Shenzhen, Guangdong

1 3 5 7 9 10 8 6 4 2

www.bloomsbury.com

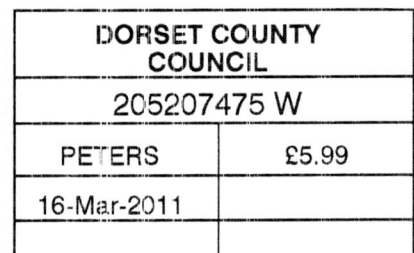

Mini Racer

Kristy Dempsey

ILLUSTRATED BY

Bridget Strevens-Marzo

BLOOMSBURY

LONDON BERLIN NEW YORK SYDNEY

round the corners, take your place.

Ready, steady. Green light, go!
Mini Racer won't move slow.

Out the gate and down the hill.
Jump a speed bump, show your skill!

Over, under, in and through.

Obstacles are tough to do.

Veer through grass,
career through sand.
Try to catch up
if you can!

Zoom forward,
Sun or rain.
High-speed action,
all terrain.

Screech! A pit stop – grab a snack,

fill 'er up, then hurry back.

Rev your motor, gather pace.

Build up speed to lead the race.

Swerve, skid, hit the brakes!

Fender bender, bumps and aches.

Caution flag – take a rest.
Fix the damage. Engine test.

Cleared for racing, back on track.
Accelerate to catch the pack.

Swing to the left, steer to the right.

Back and forth,

these turns are tight!

Surge ahead to take the lead.

Beep, beep, beep! Made for speed!

Cross the finish,
racing done!

Mini Racer
is NUMBER ONE!